D0433884

I dream of peace

Moj Vukovar!
My Vukovar!
Marija, 13
displaced from
Vukovar

I dream of peace

Images of war by children of former Yugoslavia

Preface by Vanessa Redgrave

Introduction by James P. Grant, Executive Director, UNICEF

HarperCollins*Publishers*

Preface

The drawings and writings in this book are by children in schools and refugee camps throughout former Yugoslavia, some of which I visited myself during the autumn of 1993. This creative work is part of UNICEF's emergency program to help address the psychological needs of children forced to live in the midst of war.

The thoughts and feelings of these children are a powerful affirmation of both their pain and their resilience. They are also proof that the hatred and violence the children have experienced can be overcome if, and only if, we listen to them, and give every practical and professional assistance we can to the child specialists, teachers, and parents working and living with them.

The words and pictures take us on a journey through former Yugoslavia, into the hearts and minds of children whose world has been destroyed by ethnic hatred and unspeakable violence.

Dear reader, take plenty of time to look at the drawings as well as to think about what these children have written. The first chapter, "Cruel war," shows the conflict in all its inhuman details. "The day they killed my house" reveals how the children were forced to abandon everything they knew and everybody they needed—for detention centers, hospitals, or exile. "My nightmare" lays bare the wounds that cannot be seen or talked about. "When I close my eyes, I dream of peace" completes the journey. These words, spoken by fourteen-year-old Aleksandar as he was lying in a hospital bed after being severely burned by a Molotov cocktail, are proof of the extraordinary courage of these children as well as their enduring love of life.

This book is therefore a strong protest against the violation of these children's minds, bodies, and lives—a violation of their right to grow up in a world without war, regardless of where they live or who their parents are. We must listen to the messages of the only peace makers, the only future we have—the children—and we must act accordingly.

—Vanessa Redgrave
Special Representative
for the Performing Arts
UK Committee for UNICEF
January 1994

Introduction

Wars used to be fought between soldiers and on the battlefield. But today, more than ever before in history, cities and towns are the battlefield and children the victims. The trend to systematically make children targets of atrocities reflects a retrogression in human behavior.

In former Yugoslavia, harming children has become a strategy of war. During several visits there, I saw firsthand the impact of the conflict upon the young. The war is a world of darkness where children hunt for food, dodging mortars and snipers' bullets. It is a place where the best of friends can turn into arch enemies overnight.

When young Aleksandar in Sarajevo, severely burned in an explosion, said, "When I close my eyes, I dream of peace," he was expressing the fervent hope of all the children of former Yugoslavia. The title of this book is a tribute to Aleksandar's dream.

I dream of peace is a testament both to the horrors that Aleksandar and other children are enduring—and to the extraordinary hope that burns so brightly within them. It is also a passionate appeal by children whose right to a normal life has been taken away and whose cries for peace have so far gone unheard. Their drawings and writings are silent reminders of the unspeakable atrocities that afflict their daily lives.

In these pages, the children deliver a serious message to adults: *Understand the cruelties of this war and what it is doing to us, your children! Do whatever it takes to end it! Take our child's-eye view of the promises and possibilities of peace!*

The four chapters in this book encapsulate how children in former Yugoslavia are being helped through art therapy and counselling to heal some of the traumas of war. In the first three chapters, the children, through their art, poems, and letters, confront and deal with their war experiences by expressing their anguish. In the final chapter, in a kaleidoscope of hopeful messages and drawings, they celebrate their desire for peace and friendship.

The drawing titled *War,* by Zvonimir, shows the destruction of villages and asks us to comprehend the criminality of such action. In Mario's monster drawing, titled *Fear*, we see how the daily traumas of war become a child's nightmares. In a poem, ten-year-old Roberto asks grown-ups to join him in creating a world in which "tanks would be playhouses for the kids...and all the world's children would sleep in a peace unbroken by alerts or by shooting."

These drawings and poems bring to mind Aristophanes' play *Lysistrata*, in which the women rose up collectively and demanded peace. Now it is the children's turn and *I dream of peace* is their call to action.

With the conflict entering its third year, the dimensions of the horror remain shocking. According to the International War Crimes Tribunal, established to investigate violations of humanitarian law in former Yugoslavia, women and the young and the old have been singled out for the most brutal treatment as a strategy of ethnic cleansing. So far, the war has created nearly four million refugees, of whom more than 600,000 are children. An estimated 15,000 children have died. Many more have been gravely injured.

The mind reels at the notion that anyone could deliberately target a child. That the killing, maiming, and psychological brutalizing of young children is allowed to continue in former Yugoslavia is simply unconscionable. It is a particular embarrassment to the world community. In September 1990, government leaders met at United Nations Headquarters in New York to participate in the first-ever World Summit for Children. There they signed a declaration on the survival, protection, and development of children that committed them to concrete plans of action. The Convention on the Rights of the Child, which codifies sweeping protections for the young, came into effect at the same time.

But "the rights of the child" is a cruel joke to children who have seen their houses shattered and their loved ones killed and crippled. For those who experience such all-encompassing conflict, feelings of anxiety, fear, and guilt become overwhelming. As a result, the incidence of psychological distress—or what is now known as post-traumatic stress disorder (PTSD)—soars.

UNICEF, working on all sides of the conflict in coordination with the rest of the United Nations system and relief organizations, has responded to this crisis by training local professionals and volunteers to define the symptoms of PTSD, identify its victims, and offer group and individual psychotherapy. In addition, UNICEF is helping to educate parents and the public about how to prevent long-term psychological damage.

The trauma can last for weeks, months, even years, and can manifest itself in psychosomatic disorders, anxiety, and depression. Severe behavioral problems can emerge in the children, including aggression, social withdrawal, and difficulty in concentrating and sleeping. We now know that the aftereffects of traumatic events can last even longer than a lifetime, transmitted by parents to their children, and so continuing the bitter cycle of hatred.

War and violence-induced trauma are not irreversible. Psychosocial trauma can be treated and lasting damage prevented. The prognosis for children is especially heartening. Psychologically more adaptive to change than adults, children respond more readily to treatment. But getting the treatment to them as rapidly as possible is crucial. It is most effective in the first few weeks after a traumatic experience, particularly if the children are in loving environments with parents and other adults. Helping the children express their emotions and externalize their fears and worries is essential to alleviating the trauma. Preventing them from sharing their feelings and experiences only pushes the emotional pain deeper and causes problems later.

The drawings and writings in this book represent the healing process at work for some of the war-traumatized children of former Yugoslavia. In dozens of schools and refugee camps throughout the region, children have been encouraged to draw and write as a way to unlock the doors to their inner emotions. Assisted by parents, teachers, psychologists, and art therapists, the children recall not only traumatic events but also happy memories from the past. They also create promising dreams of the future.

We at UNICEF support this undertaking because of our growing concern for the mental health of children in wartime—a concern as pressing as our traditional focus on providing food, shelter, safe water, sanitation, and protection from disease. UNICEF has also helped war-traumatized children in Cambodia, El Salvador, Lebanon, Liberia, Mozambique, the Sudan, and other countries. Simple therapeutic treatments have been devised and taught to local professionals and volunteers. They have proven effective in helping large numbers of children with PTSD.

Gradually, these methods have been systematized and standardized. For example, during the Persian Gulf War, a coordinated effort was mounted to collect information on the incidence of PTSD in Kuwait and Iraq, identify the most severe cases and build popular support for programs that address the long-term needs of PTSD victims. UNICEF also participates in initiatives aimed at creating lasting peace, such as post-conflict programs in Lebanon and Mozambique. Our purpose is to help change values and build interfaith understanding and tolerance among children from all sides of the conflict so they come to embrace each other as brothers and sisters.

But in former Yugoslavia, peace is as yet only a distant dream. This book is the children's rallying cry—a wake-up call for all of us to understand their plight. I urge you to go through it page by page. Imagine what it is like to be these children. Share their fear, their sorrow, and their hope. Then join them in their quest by using this book to promote peace. Let us try to establish zones of peace—conflict-free oases where children can be protected from war. Let us try to rally politicians and world leaders to forge a lasting peace in the region. Let us do everything in our power to put an end to the horror and to help the children realize their dreams of peace.

—James P. Grant
Executive Director, UNICEF
December 1993

I am speaking to you, the one they forced from the playground and from the street, from the house where you lived and from your childhood room.

As you suffer, I suffer, and my nights are sleepless too. I swear to you, I do not kick the football like before, I do not sing the way I did. I have locked up my bicycle, and I have locked up my smile. I have locked up my games and my childish jokes as well.

Will the waiting be long? I do not want to grow old while still just a child, and I fear for you that, in the wait, the place of your birth will soon be forgotten. Therefore, my friend, welcome to my place. We will share the sea, and the beauty of a summer evening. We will enjoy the singing of the birds and do our homework together.

—Nemanja, 11, from Sutomore

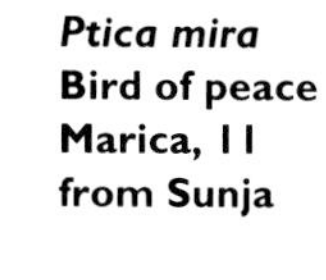

Ptica mira
Bird of peace
Marica, 11
from Sunja

Cruel war

Rat
War
Robert, 14
refugee from Foča

Wiiiiiuuuuu
VATROGASNI DOM

A grenade had landed on our shelter. We had to climb over the dead bodies to get out. Meanwhile the snipers kept shooting at us.

My father was one of those wounded and was taken away to the hospital. We've not seen him since, but I hope that he is still alive, perhaps in one of the detention camps.

I try not to talk about these things, but I get so upset and keep having nightmares about what happened.

—Kazimir, 13, displaced

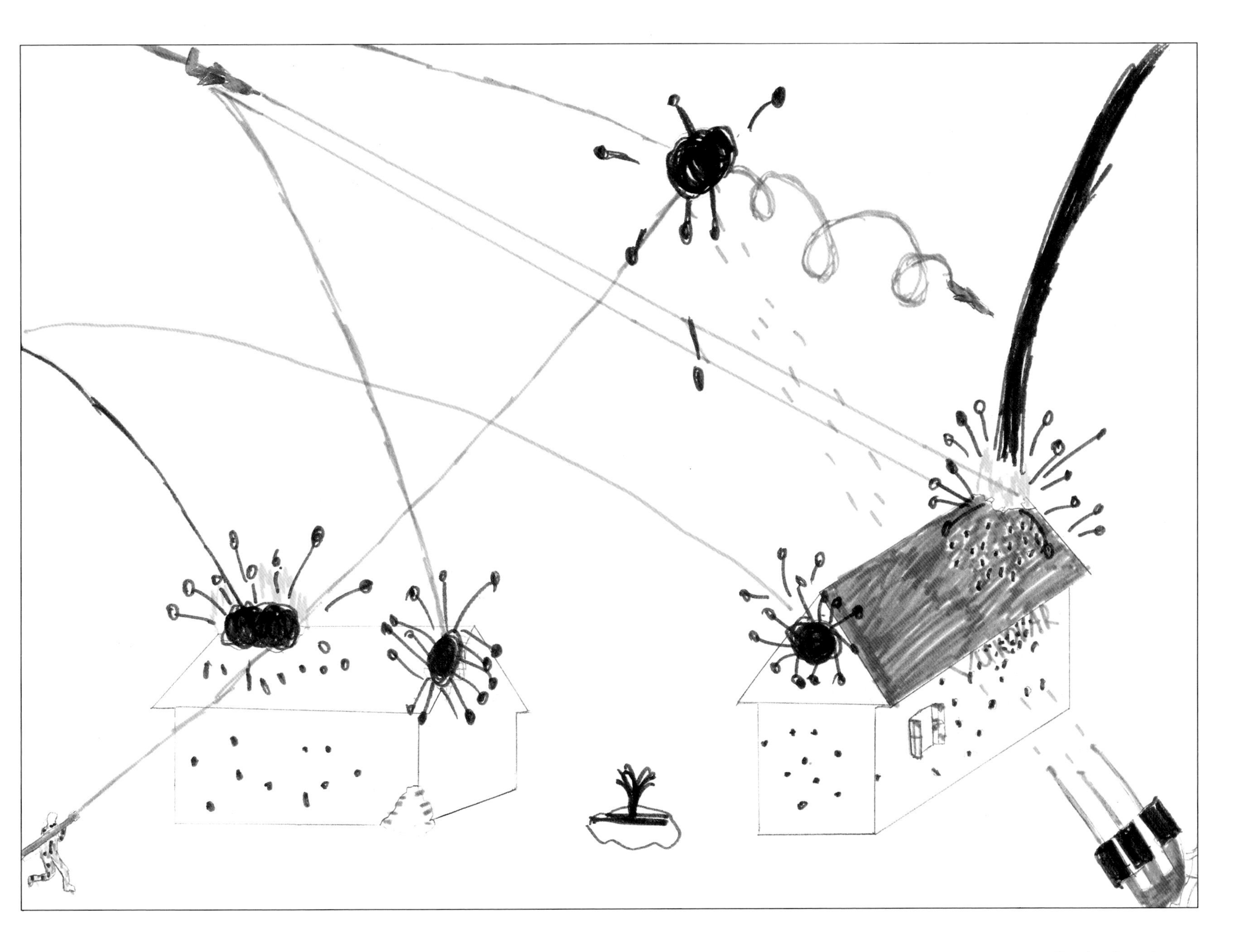

Bombardovanje
Bombardment
Mario, 10
from Stari Mikanovci

Bitka
The battle
Mirko, 11
displaced from Tenja, near Vukovar

Rat
War
Zvonimir, 12
from Požega

I am not a refugee, but I understand the fear and the suffering of the children.

My father is a Croat, my mother is a Serb, but I don't know who I am.

My brothers, my sisters, my grandparents, my aunts, and my uncles, all are in Croatia. I have not seen them since the start of this horrible war.

More than a year has passed since I heard their voices. And the only link between us are the letters, letters, only letters....

—Lepa, 11, from Belgrade

Uspomene
Memories
Tihomir, 12
refugee from Buna, near Mostar

PAD CERIĆA

Pad Cerića
Fall of Cerić
Mario, 11
displaced from Cerić

Tata, ne idi u rat
Daddy, don't go to war
Ratko, 14
displaced from Lipik

If only you knew how it feels to have your father in the war. You flee the misery, but misery follows. You hear not a word about your father, and one day everything goes black and there is Daddy at the door. He stays with you a few days and then happiness is gone again.

My heart, it is pounding like a little clock. I can hardly write this because my beloved Daddy is once again not here with me.

—Žana, 12, refugee from Brčko

САМО ДА РАТА
НЕ БУДЕ

Samo da rata ne bude
If only there wasn't a war
Danilo, 11
from Šabac

Stop the war and the fighting
for a smile on a child's face.
Stop the planes and the shells
for a smile on a child's face.

Stop all the army vehicles
for a smile on a child's face.
Stop everything that kills and destroys
for a smile of happiness on a child's face.

—Ivana, 11, from Čepin

It's all so strange! Suddenly, it's so important, everybody asking who you are, what you do, where you come from.

So many people have been killed fighting for justice. But what justice? Do they know what they are fighting for, who they are fighting?

The weather is growing very cold now. No longer can you hear the singing of the birds, only the sound of the children crying for a lost mother or father, a brother or a sister.

We are children without a country and without hope.

—Dunja, 14, from Belgrade

Rat
War
Amela, 12
displaced from
Slavonski Brod

The day they killed my house

Mama, čekaj me!
Mama, wait for me!
Hrvoje, 11
from Zagreb

We stayed five months at my grandmother's house. There was quite a lot of shelling, air raids, and general alerts. So many buildings were burned down, and every house was hit by at least one shell.

Mak and I slept on the floor, and mother and father on a couch. We had little to eat, only rice, spaghetti, and sometimes beans. We didn't have any other vegetables, only one tomato cut in three pieces for Mak, Deni, and me....

We all lost weight except for Asja. She doesn't get any humanitarian aid, but she eats ours. Poor thing, she never goes out to exercise, but still she is happier than other dogs who have lost their masters.

—Lana, 8, from Sarajevo

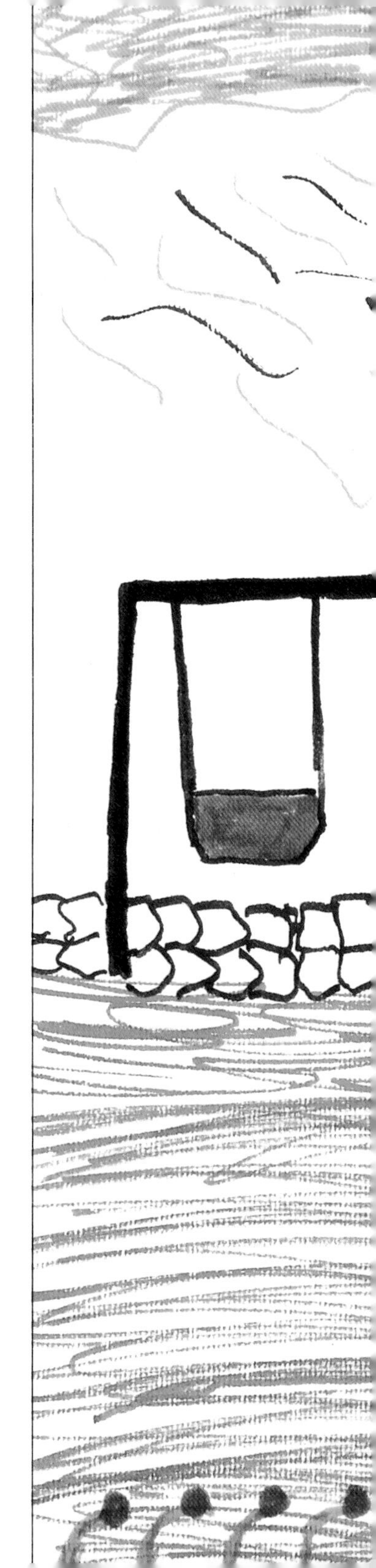

Bez naslova
Untitled
Matteya, 12
from Moščenica

My sister and I were refugees who fled from Moščenica. We stayed in Zagorje with our grandmother. She was always anxious and constantly yelling at us. Day after day, night after night, we waited for our mother to join us. But she never arrived.

One day, I was sitting on the steps of my house when a blue car came down the street. Inside, I saw my mother. I flew toward her, and then I hugged her to me.

When she said that we would be going back home to Moščenica, I was filled with happiness. However, when we arrived there, many of the houses were destroyed, and the sight left me heartsick.

I couldn't believe there could ever be life in our town again. Anyone who saw the destruction would feel the same. That is why this dirty war must stop.

—Jelena, 11, from Moščenica

Progon djece iz Slavonskog Broda
Children forced to leave
Slavonski Brod
Stjepan, 12
displaced from Slavonski Brod

SLAVONIJA TRANS
SLAV. BROD

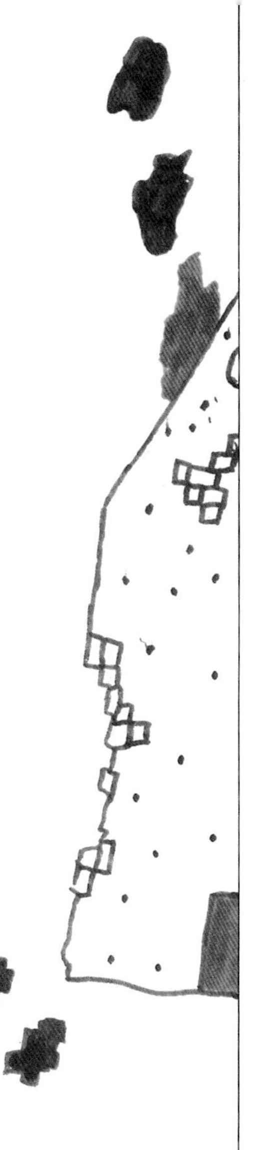

I had a new tricycle, red and yellow and with a bell....Do you think they have destroyed my tricycle too?

—*Nedim, 5, refugee*

Razrušene kuće i drveće
Destroyed houses and trees
Mario, 10
displaced from Sotin

Razrušeni grad
Destroyed city
Ružica, 13
from Đakovački Selci

Strava i užas
Horror and scream
Dinko, 12
from Požega

War is the saddest word that flows from my quivering lips. It is a wicked bird that never comes to rest. It is a deadly bird that destroys our homes, and deprives us of our childhood. War is the evilest of birds, turning the streets red with blood, and the world into an inferno.

—*Maida, 12, from Skopje*

This is the worst memory in my heart....I wouldn't want anyone to experience it. The women and children are being taken away by force to the detention camp. I can't get the picture out of my head because I've experienced it myself.

—Mario, 13, from Dubrovnik

Nasilno odvođenje žena i djece u logor
Women and children forced into detention camp
Mario, 13
from Dubrovnik

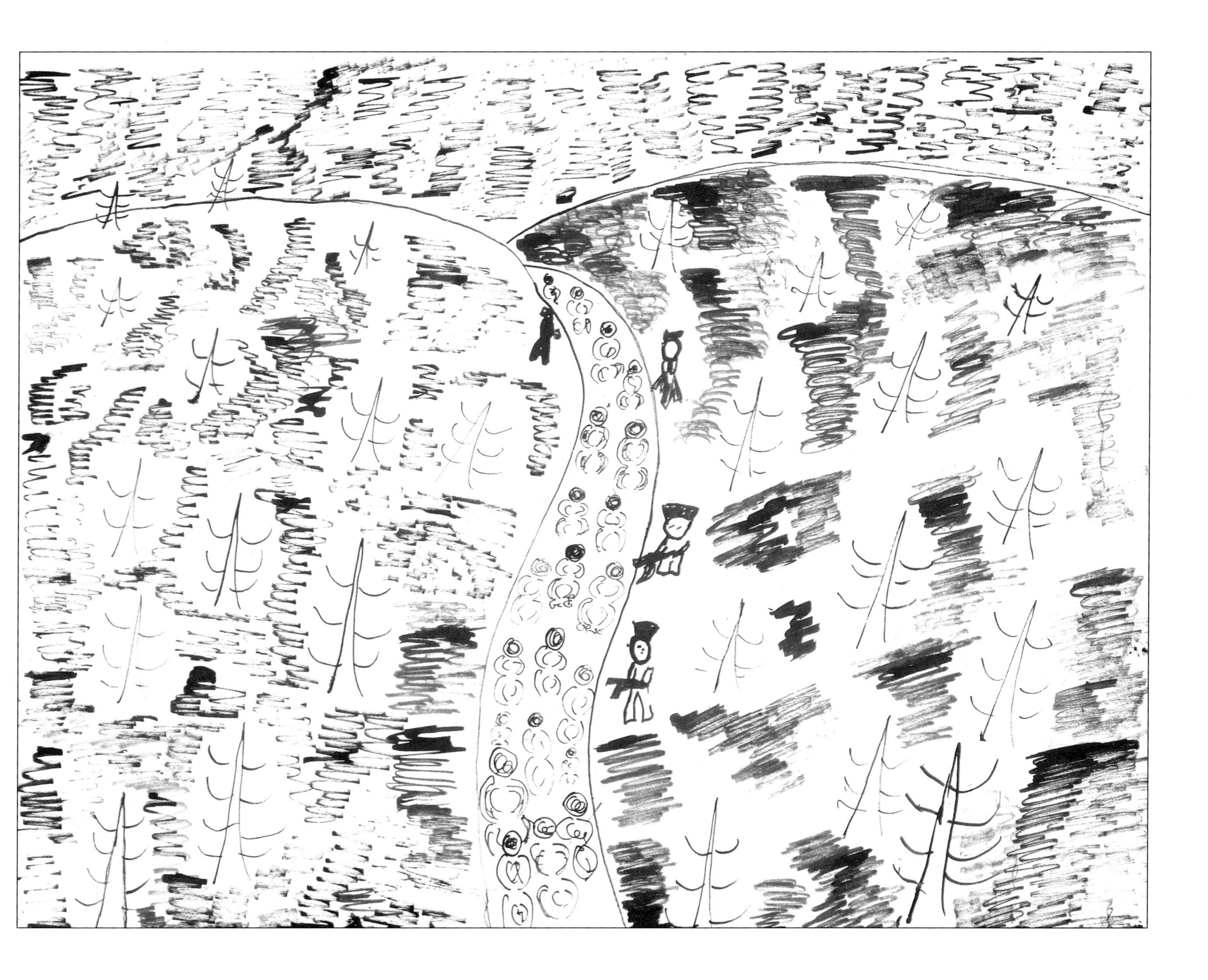

Majka i dijete
Mother and child
Ankica, 11
from Požega

U logoru
In detention camp
Marinela, 12
from Čepin

Ranjena djeca u bolnici
Wounded children in hospital
Suzana, 14
from Donji Miholjac

In my dreams, I walk among the ruins
of the old part of town
looking for a bit of stale bread.

My mother and I inhale the fumes of gunpowder.
I imagine it to be the smell of pies, cakes, and kebab.

A shot rings out from a nearby hill. We hurry.
Though it's only nine o'clock, we might be hurrying
toward a grenade marked "ours."

An explosion rings out in the street of dignity.
Many people are wounded—
sisters, brothers, mothers, fathers.

I reach out to touch a trembling, injured hand.
I touch death itself.

Terrified, I realize this is not a dream.
It is just another day in Sarajevo.

—Edina, 12, from Sarajevo

Hodanje po ruševinama
Walking in ruins
Robert, 13
refugee from Kotor Varoš

My nightmare

Strah
Fear
Mario, 11
from Požega

Strah u meni
Fear in me
Jovana, 6
from Belgrade

Bez naslova
Untitled
Artist unknown

Rođena sam da patim
I was born to suffer
Žana, 12
refugee from Brčko

I remember going to our apartment during an alert. When I entered the corridor, all the doors were closed. Slowly, I walked through the dark and opened the bedroom door. All at once, the sun shone brightly upon me. My sadness and fear completely vanished. But while I was enjoying it, I felt as if I had no right to such happiness.

—*Ivan, 13, refugee from Tuzla*

Duhovi i skeleti u mome ormaru
Ghosts and skeletons in my closet
Adrijana, 12
from Požega

When I walk through town, I see strange faces, full of bitterness and pain. Where has our laughter gone? Where is our happiness? Somewhere far, far away from us. Why did they do this to us? We're their kids. All we want is to play our games and see our friends. And not to have this horrible war.

There are so many people who did not ask for this war, or for the black earth that is now over them. Among them are my friends.

I send you this message: Don't ever hurt the children. They're not guilty of anything.

—Sandra, 10, from Vukovar

Očekivali smo samo bonbone
We were only waiting for candies
Belma, 10
from Sarajevo

Belma IV2

The soldiers ordered us out of our house and then burned it down. After that, they took us to the train, where they ordered all the men to lie down on the ground.

From the group, they chose the ones they were going to kill. They picked my uncle and a neighbor! Then they machine-gunned them to death. After that, the soldiers put the women in the front cars of the train and the men in the back. As the train started moving, they disconnected the back cars and took the men off and to the camps. I saw it all!

Now I can't sleep. I try to forget, but it doesn't work. I have such difficulty feeling anything anymore.

—Alik, 13, refugee

Moj najveći strah
My worst fear
Marija, 12
refugee from
Bosanski Brod

Dlakavo čudovište
Hairy monster
Oliver, 12
from Požega

When I close my eyes
I dream of peace

Bez naslova
Untitled
Predrag, 12
from Belgrade

War is here, but we await peace. We are in a corner of the world where nobody seems to hear us. But we are not afraid, and we will not give up.

Our fathers earn little, just barely enough to buy five kilos of flour a month. And we have no water, no electricity, no heat. We bear it all, but we cannot bear the hate and the evil.

Our teacher has told us about Anne Frank, and we have read her diary. After fifty years, history is repeating itself right here with this war, with the hate and the killing, and with having to hide to save your life.

We are only twelve years old. We can't influence politics and the war, but we want to live! And we want to stop this madness. Like Anne Frank fifty years ago, we wait for peace. She didn't live to see it. Will we?

—Students from a fifth-grade class in Zenica

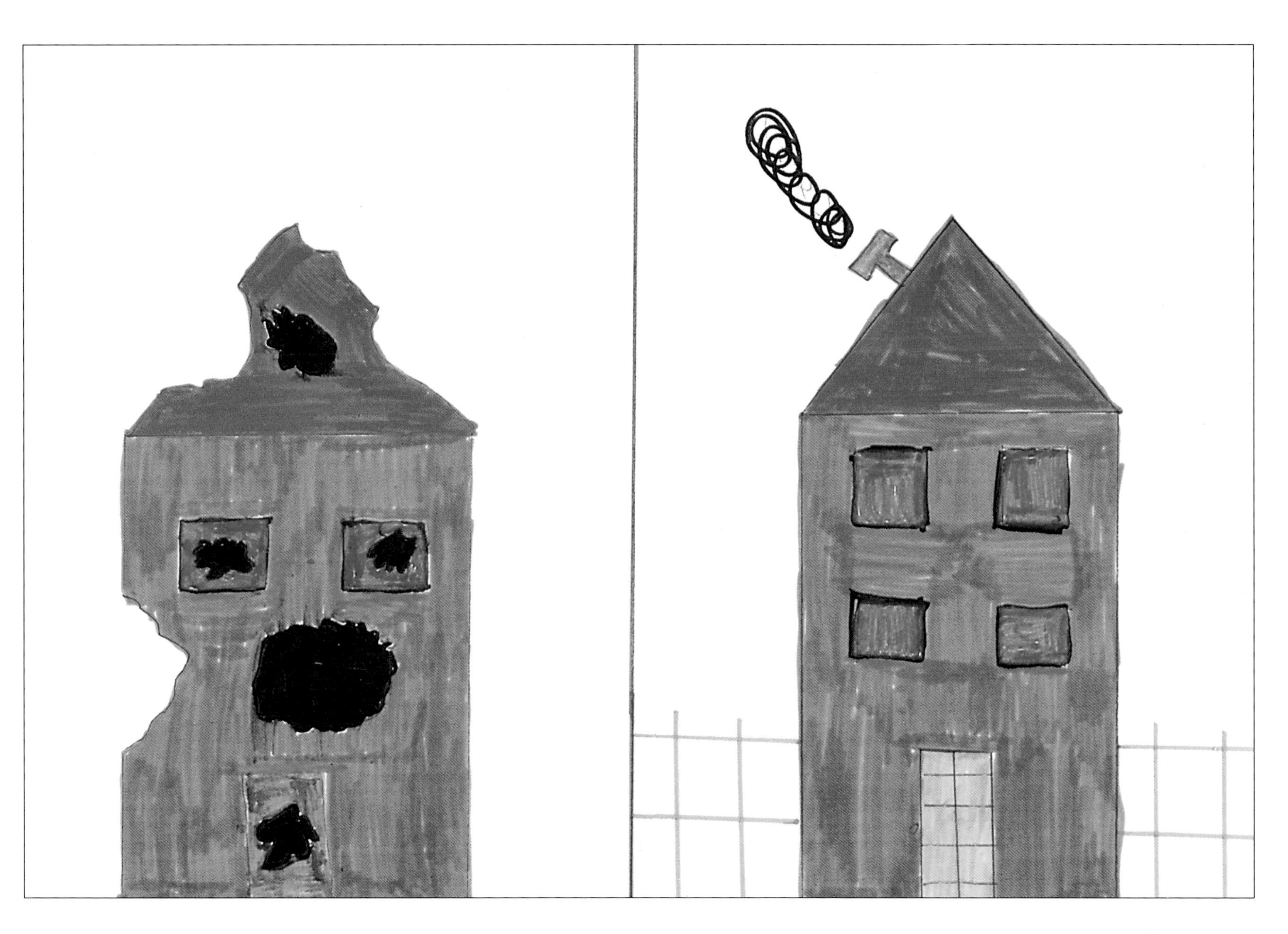

Rat i mir
War and peace
Nataša, 11
from Pula

Ja sam ptica mira i želim
da ovaj rat što prije završi.
I da se svi slažu u tuzi,
u sreći, u ljubavi i u miru
Danijela!

Poruka svijetu
Message to the world
Danijela, 11
refugee from Derventa

My wish list

Jeans: Levis 501
Sneakers: Reeboks
Coat: a college jacket
Shoes: cowboy boots

—Jozo, 12
from Vukovar

Moj san
My dream
Nikola and Aleksandar
from Belgrade

Mir i ljubav
Peace and love
Marta and Ana, 9
from Belgrade

МИР
М
М
ЉУБАВ
М
Марта и Ана

If I were President,
the tanks would be playhouses for the kids.
Boxes of candy would fall from the sky.
The mortars would fire balloons.
And the guns would blossom with flowers.

All the world's children
would sleep in a peace unbroken
by alerts or by shooting.

The refugees would return to their villages.
And we would start anew.

—Roberto, 10, from Pula

Poruke
Messages
Maja, 12
from Požega

To all children throughout the world

I want you to know our suffering, the children of Sarajevo. I am still young, but I feel that I have experienced things that many grown-ups will never know. I don't mean to upset you, but I want you to know that I was staying in Serbian-held territory when my mother and I were put on the list and marked for liquidation. Those of you who live normal lives can't understand such things, nor could I, until I experienced them.

While you are eating your fruit and your sweet chocolate and candy, over here we are plucking grass to survive. When you next have some tasty food, please say to yourself, "This is for the children of Sarajevo."

While you are at the cinema or listening to beautiful music, we are scurrying into basements, and listening to the terrible whine of cannon shells. While you are laughing and having fun, we are crying and hoping that this terror will quickly pass. While you are enjoying the benefits of electricity and running water, and having your baths, we are praying to God for rain so we can have some water to drink.

No film can adequately depict the suffering, the fear, and the terror that my people are experiencing. Sarajevo is awash in blood, and graves are appearing everywhere. I beg you in the name of the Bosnian children never to allow this to happen to you or to people anywhere else.

—Edina, 12, from Sarajevo

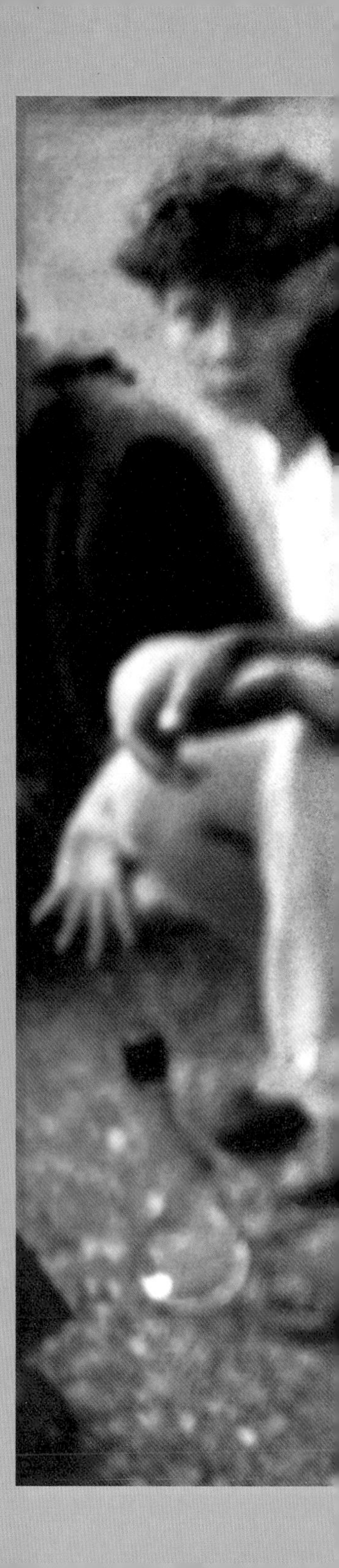

Acknowledgments

UNICEF extends its warmest thanks to the children, and the psychologists, teachers, and parents who assisted them, in all regions of former Yugoslavia who have made this book possible.

We wish to acknowledge the contributions of Edith Simmons, who conceived the book while Information Officer in the UNICEF Area Office for former Yugoslavia (Zagreb); Rune Stuvland, Psychosocial Advisor at UNICEF Zagreb, for his valuable advice; and Thomas McDermott, UNICEF Special Representative in former Yugoslavia, and his colleagues in Belgrade, Sarajevo, and Zagreb.

This project could not have been completed without the support of colleagues at the Division of Information, UNICEF Headquarters, New York: Ellen Tolmie, Photo Editor, whose commitment and hard work saw the project to completion; Shalini Dewan, Chief of Editorial, Publications, and Photo Section, who oversaw the editorial process; and Mehr Khan, Director, who provided overall guidance.

Special thanks also to Stephanie Allen-Early, Sonja Bičanić, Joost Bloemsma, Tia Bruer, Clayton Carlson, Robert Cohen, Karen Dautresme, Brigitte Duchesne, Richard Gorman, Amy Janello, Brennon Jones, James Mohan, Branka Palešćak, Fran Scott, Carl Taylor, Thomas Walker, and Sherri Whitmarsh.

We also thank the international agent for *I dream of peace*, Linda Michaels, and subagents Ann-Christine Danielsson and Hiroko Kuroda.

The first edition of *I dream of peace* was published simultaneously by Editorial Atlántida, Argentina; Bertelsmann, Germany; Editions du Chêne, France; Ediciones Folio, Spain; Gyldendal Norsk Forlag, Norway; HarperCollins Publishers, USA, Canada, UK, Australia, New Zealand; Holp Shuppan, Japan; Rabén och Sjögren, Sweden; Forlaget Sesam, Denmark; Uitgeverij Het Spectrum, Netherlands; and Standaard Uitgeverij, Belgium.

Photography credits: page 4—Senad Gubelić; page 6—Senad Gubelić; page 75—Darko Gorenak; page 76 (clockwise from top left)—Senad Gubelić; UNICEF/5134/John Isaac; Marc de Haan; Senad Gubelić; page 77 (clockwise from top left)—Marc de Haan; Marc de Haan; Marc de Haan; UNICEF/5131/John Isaac; page 78—Marc de Haan; page 80—UNICEF/5132/John Isaac.

First published throughout the world in the English language in 1994 by
HarperCollins Publishers, Inc., 10 East 53rd Street, New York, NY 10022

Produced by Jones & Janello, New York
Designed by GRAF/x, New York
Color separations by RCA Zwolle, the Netherlands
Printed by Aubin Imprimeur, Poitiers, France

ISBN 0-06-251128-9
94 95 96 97 98 AI 10 9 8 7 6 5 4 3 2 1
FIRST EDITION